Fussbum Series.

Fussbum
Goes on a Bike Ride

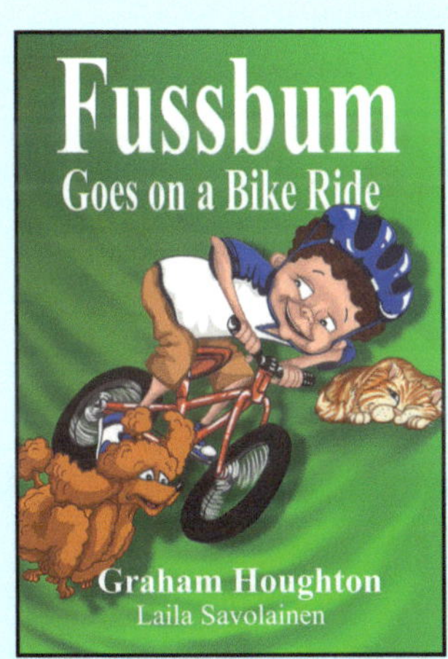

Graham Houghton
Laila Savolainen

National Library of Australia Cataloguing-in-Publication entry
Creator: Houghton, Graham D., author.
Title: Fussbum goes on a bike ride / Graham Houghton ; Laila Savolainen.
ISBN: 9780994344700 (paperback).
ISBN: 9780994344717 (ebook).
Series: Houghton, Graham D. Fussbum series ; bk. 1.
Target Audience: For primary school age.
Subjects: Boys--Juvenile fiction.
   Cycling--Juvenile fiction.
   Adventure stories.
   Imagination in children--Juvenile fiction.
   Play--Juvenile fiction.
Other Creators/Contributors: Savolainen, Laila Kristina, 1967- illustrator.
Dewey Number: A823.4.

Publishing Details
Published in Australia – Wagtail Publications
www.fussbum.com.au

Publishing Consultants
Design and artwork supplied: Pickawoowoo Publishing Group

Printed & Channel Distribution
Lightning Source / Ingram

For my beautiful grandchildren
Ariyana, Ethan, Julian and Sebastian...

for making my life as a 'Grandad' so much fun
and full of so many happy memories.

Fussbum's off on another bike ride

with Puddles his dog by his side.

Puddles is a poncy little poodle

with a pom-pom on his tail

and a pom-pom on his noodle.

Scratch the cat,
who sleeps with

one eye open,
crawls into bushes to watch.

"Running around is not for me.
I'm a slinking cat.
Saving the energy I need

to jump on a feed."

Fussbum pumped the pedals.

Pedal, pedal, pedal,

vroom, vroom, vroom.

He thinks, just the bike and me.

Not a care in the world.

I'm free, free, free.

Off like a rocket he shot.

Out through the gate

and onto the path.

His backside was all that

Puddles could see.

But as the bike sped away

it began to sway.

On the path was a mum pushing a pram.
Fussbum yelled "scram" as the bike whizzed
past with a wobble, wobble, wobble.

"Hey watch out" called the lady
with a splutter,

"Your wobbly bike nearly
pushed my pram into the gutter."

Children were playing on the path.

But Fussbum was going too fast.

"Scatter" he yelled as he went past.

Puddles looked in dismay as Fussbum

broke up their play.

"He should take more care.

This path is for all to share."

Old Gran had lived near the path all
her life. And her daily walk was
part of her life.
She'd stagger and totter all over the
place, and waggle her walking stick
right in your face.

She spied Fussbum going too fast.

She stuck out her stick.

"He'll not get past."

"Hey young Fussbum" she cried, "this path
is for all to share. You're being a bully
and not playing fair.

Repairs
Under
Way

"And watch out. The path up ahead
is under repair. There's bits dug up
and potholes everywhere."
But Fussbum had his head in the air
watching a bird flying here and there.
If birds can fly then why can't I.

When suddenly - CRUNCH - he hit a pothole.

Over went the bike and off flew Fussbum.

But he couldn't fly and he landed KERPLOP.

He landed upside down in another pothole.

With his head where his bum should be,

and his bum where his head should be.

Repairs
Under
Way

Up ponced Puddles with a giggle.

"He's an upside down Fussbum" said Puddles.

"He's turned into a Bumfuss."

"Stop giggling and get help" said Fussbum,

"I'm stuck."

Puddles ponced off and soon was in luck,

for passing close by was Constable Cop.

"Just as well you were wearing your helmet"
he said.

"But you've been a naughty lad.
You've been riding your bike real bad.
You've frightened the children,
pushed a mum with a pram, and strewth,
you've even upset Old Gran."

"Riding your bike is fun" said Constable Cop.

"But the path is for all to share.

Be aware and

show more care."

Fussbum had learnt his lesson. As he rode

home he played with the children, said hello

to the lady with the pram and

waved to Old Gran.